MW01179024

Won't Papa Be Surprised!

For Jody and Ross with love.
Without you, how could I be a mom?
—T.C.

For my daughter, Jessica, a splendid model
—E.S.

Won't Papa Be Surprised!
Text copyright © 2003 by Terri Cohlene
Illustrations copyright © 2003 by Elizabeth Sayles
Manufactured in China. All rights reserved.
www.harperchildrens.com

Library of Congress Cataloging-in-Publication Data
Cohlene, Terri, date.
Won't papa be surprised! / by Terri Cohlene ; illustrated by Elizabeth Sayles.
p.   cm.
Summary: Mikele's gift for Papa on Father's Day makes her think about and see ribbons
everywhere, but her father has his own surprise for her.
ISBN 0-688-13093-3 — ISBN 0-688-13094-1 (lib. bdg.)
[1. Fathers and daughters—Fiction. 2. Father's Day—Fiction. 3. Ribbons—Fiction.] I. Sayles,
Elizabeth, ill. II. Title.
PZ7.C6648 Ri 2003
[Fic]—dc21
2002024024
CIP
AC

Typography by Jeanne L. Hogle

1 2 3 4 5 6 7 8 9 10
❖
First Edition

Won't Papa Be Surprised!

by Terri Cohlene

illustrated by Elizabeth Sayles

HarperCollinsPublishers

Sunlight streamed through the shutters and bounced off the kitchen wall. Like ribbons, thought Mikele, sunshine ribbons especially for today.

Papa drizzled cream over their oatmeal, and Mikele tapped out the cinnamon. "Lots to do this morning," Papa said.

Mikele ate as fast as she could. I can hardly wait till chores are done, she thought. Won't Papa be surprised!

After breakfast Mikele helped Papa in the garden. He pulled dandelions while she filled her basket with purple clover.

She twisted some of the blossoms together
and tied them around her neck. Like ribbons,
she thought, flowery ribbons.

"Are we done yet, Papa?" she asked.

"Not yet," he answered.

Next they fixed the wiggly front step.

Papa held the nails while Mikele pounded

them in.

Then he lifted her onto his shoulders and handed her the wind sock. It was shaped like a fish. As she hung it from the rafters, the breeze picked up the tail streamers and flipped them into the air. Mikele smiled. Like ribbons, she thought, flippety ribbons.

"Are we done yet, Papa?" she asked.

"Not yet," he answered. "Let's wash the car."

Papa washed up high, and Mikele washed down low.

Then she rinsed the tires. She rinsed Papa too.

He laughed and squirted her feet.

Then Mikele made watery loops with the hose.
Like ribbons, she thought, squiggly ribbons.

"Are we done *now*, Papa?" she asked.

Papa stretched his back. "I'd say so," he said.

Mikele clapped her hands. "Will you help me
fix tea on the porch? Please, Papa?"

Papa smiled. "Good idea, sweetie."

Papa brought out the honey cakes while Mikele spread a cloth on the porch table. "Honey cakes are my favorite," she said.

"Mine too," Papa answered. "When I was your age, Gram always baked them for special days."

Twheeeeeeee! The teakettle sang, and Papa poured boiling water into the pot. Mikele added peppermint leaves and watched the steam curl into the air. Like ribbons, she thought, twirly ribbons.

Then she ran to her room and opened her
toy chest. Taking out a small package, Mikele
hurried back and slid it next to Papa's plate.
"What's this?" he asked with a wink.

"Happy Father's Day, Papa!" Mikele squealed. "Open it!"

Inside, Papa found a big purple ribbon with a badge that read MY PAPA.

"It's perfect," he said. Then he handed *her* a box. "For you, Mikele."

"But Papa," she said, "this is Father's Day. Why are you giving *me* a present?"

Papa gave her ponytail a playful tug.
"If it weren't for you, Mikele, how could I even be
a papa? Go on now, open it."

Mikele tore off the tissue paper and opened
the lid. Out sprang a tangle of satin ribbons——
lavender, pink, and periwinkle. "Oh, Papa, they're
beautiful!" she cried.

"Just like you," Papa said, and he smiled as he braided the curly ribbons into her hair.